The Grizzly Bear With the Frizzly Hair

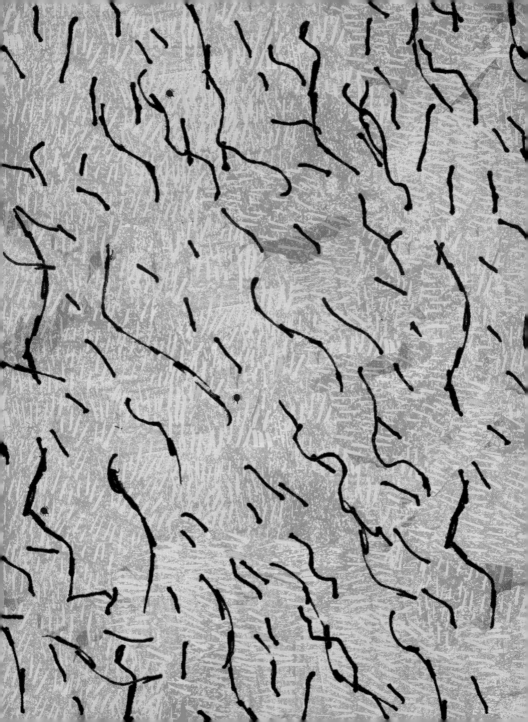

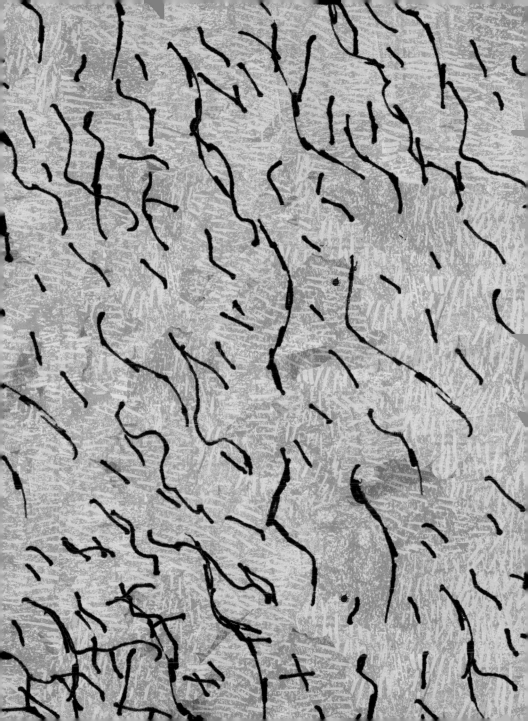

For Karen – ST

For Penny – HS

This isn't a new story. It is my retelling of a folktale which
has been around for more than 2000 years. Versions of the story
have been recorded in countries as far apart as Ireland, South Africa,
Iran, China and the USA. And I'd like to start by raising my hat
to the storytellers who passed it on to us now. S.T.

The Grizzly Bear with the Frizzly Hair © Frances Lincoln Limited 2011
Text © Sean Taylor 2011
Illustrations © Hannah Shaw 2011

The moral rights of Sean Taylor and Hannah Shaw have been asserted

First published in Great Britain and in the USA in 2012
This early reader edition published in Great Britain in 2013 by
Frances Lincoln Children's Books,
74-77 White Lion Street, London, N1 9PF
www.franceslincoln.com

ISBN 978-1-84780-475-4

Printed in China

1 3 5 7 9 8 6 4 2

Created in consultation with language and literacy
development specialist, Prue Goodwin.

The Grizzly Bear with the Frizzly Hair

Retold by
Sean Taylor

Illustrated by
Hannah Shaw

F

FRANCES LINCOLN
CHILDREN'S BOOKS

There was nothing left to eat in the woods.
The Grizzly Bear with the Frizzly Hair had eaten it all.
That's why he was bad-tempered and hungry.
That's why he was on the prowl.

The Grizzly Bear
with the Frizzly Hair

could frighten the feathers
off a peacock.

He could
startle the
whiskers off
a walrus.

He could scare the
stripes off a tiger.

So how do you think this
itzy-bitzy rabbit felt, when
they came face to face?

"Yipes!" blinked the rabbit.
"What are you going to do?"
"Have my lunch," growled the bear.
"And my lunch is . . . you!"

Then he opened his frizzly, grizzly mouth and
dangled the rabbit inside.
"You're going to eat my toes!" said the rabbit.
"Please do not! Those toes there
are the favourite ones I've got!"

"Tough!"
growled the bear.
"That's how it goes!
I'm hungry and
those look like
very tasty toes!"

He opened his frizzly, grizzly mouth a little wider.
"Not my knees!" said the rabbit. "Please!
For heaven's sake! They're ever so very bony.
And you'll get a tummy ache!"

"Hmm," growled the bear, "I don't care if I do!
They'll make a lovely crunching sound
every time I chew!"

"Not my tum-tum-tummy!" said the rabbit,
"or my ch-ch-chest! If you eat up those,
there'll be hardly anything left!"

"Too bad," glared the bear. "They'll make the perfect snack. And once they're down my throat, you'll never get them back!"

He opened his frizzly, grizzly
mouth a little wider.

"My head!" squeaked the rabbit.
"Wait! Not yet! Don't bite!
Eating someone's head is really not polite!"

"I'm not polite!"
roared the bear.

"I'm rude!
Everyone knows!

And I hope you've enjoyed
the story because this is
as far as it goes!"

The frizzly, grizzly mouth
started to close.

Our itzy-bitzy friend quivered down to his marrow
bone jelly. In fact, he could have just shut his eyes,
shrivelled with fright and given up.

But he didn't. "Look behind you!" he yelled.
"An elephant's coming! Look!"
"Quiet!" growled the bear.
"That's the oldest trick in the book!"

"I know a joke!" tried the rabbit.
"It's going to make you laugh!"

"No!" bristled the bear.

"I'm going to bite
you in half."

"But I'm tiny," the rabbit babbled.
"I'll be gone in one munch!
Wouldn't you, maybe, rather have
a really big lunch?"

"End of story!" snarled the bear.
"I don't want your maybes!
What do you think this is . . .
a bedtime book for babies?"

"In the river!"
said the rabbit.
"Have a look!
You'll see!

There's something
there to eat
**much, much
bigger than me!"**

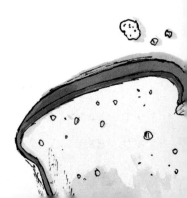

"Much, much bigger?" muttered the bear.
"Hmmmmmm." He kept a tight hold on the rabbit
but he walked back through the woods and took
a little look in the river.

What was that?
It was the strangest,
frizzliest, grizzliest thing he'd ever seen.
But it did look very filling compared to a rabbit.
"Delicious!" blinked the rabbit. "Succulent,
scrumptious and yummy! Imagine how good you'd
feel with all of that in your tummy!"

The Grizzly Bear with the Frizzly Hair dropped the
rabbit and he grabbed at the thing in the river.
But it grabbed straight back. He bared his teeth.
But it bared its teeth back.

"Oh dear!" sighed the rabbit.
"I'll tell you what I think.
It reckons you are just some
great big goofy wimp!"

The Grizzly Bear with Frizzly Hair swiped a giant paw at the thing in the river. But the thing in the river swiped a giant paw back.

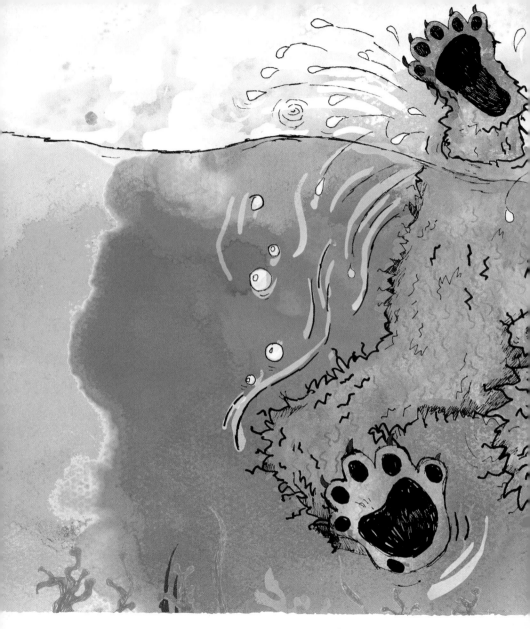

That was too much.
In a rage, the bear jumped at his own reflection.

And he sank deep down into the water.

The rabbit didn't hang about. He went skittling off as fast as he could. **"Come back!"** gurgled the bear, wrinkling his soggy nose.

"I hope you enjoyed the story," called the rabbit, "Because this is as far as it goes!"

And with that he was gone,
safely into the long grass,
checking his toes,
checking his knees,
checking his tummy,
his chest and his head.

And they were all still there!

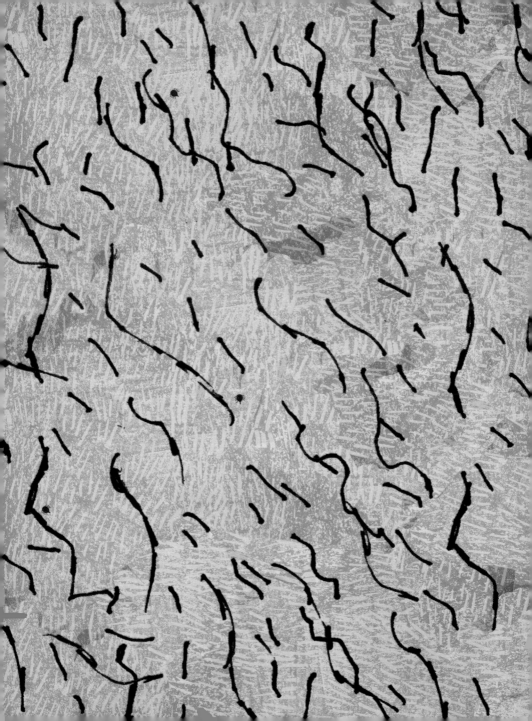

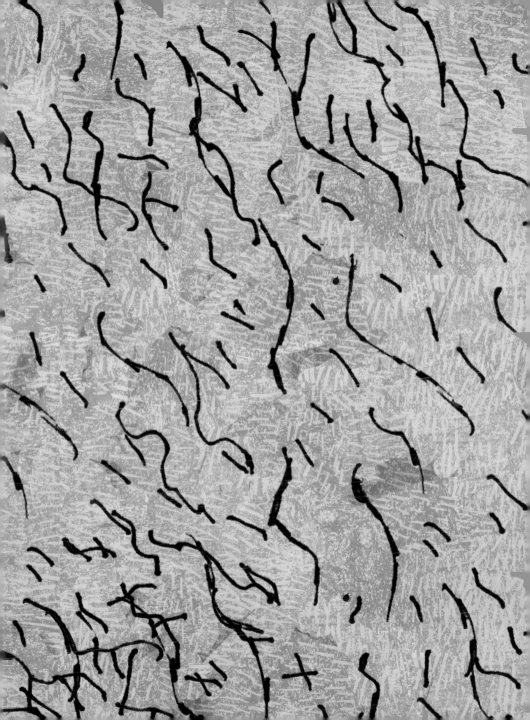

More great TIME TO READ books to collect:

978-1-84780-476-1

978-1-84780-475-4

978-1-84780-477-8

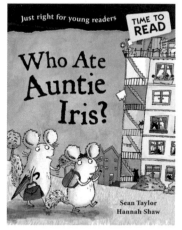

978-1-84780-478-5

Frances Lincoln titles are available from all good bookshops.
You can also buy books and find out more about your favourite titles,
authors and illustrators on our website: www.franceslincoln.com